To the Children at the Lake
Who may One Day reach the Sea
— P.K. Page

To Janet Lunn with sincere friendship
— Laszlo Gal

Oxford University Press, 70 Wynford Drive, Don Mills, Ontario, M3C 1J9

Toronto Oxford New York Delhi Bombay Calcutta Madras Karachi
Petaling Jaya Singapore Hong Kong Tokyo Nairobi Dar es Salaam
Cape Town Melbourne Auckland
and associated companies in
Berlin Ibadan

CANADIAN CATALOGUING IN PUBLICATION DATA
Page, P. K. (Patricia Kathleen), 1916-
A flask of sea water
ISBN 0-19-540704-0

I. Gal, Laszlo. II. Title.
PS8531.A43F58 1989   jC813'.54   C89-093115-1
PZ7.P334Fl 1989

A
FLASK
OF
SEA WATER

P.K. Page

Illustrated by Laszlo Gal

OXFORD UNIVERSITY PRESS 1989

I

Once upon a time in the mountainous, land-locked Kingdom of Ure, there lived a Goatherd. And every morning when the dew lay in the valley, he drove his goats up to the high meadows where the air was clear and the grass was sweet. And every evening when the sun dropped behind the topmost peaks of the westerly mountains, he drove them down to the valley again. And the months passed, and the years, as peaceful and happy as the Goatherd himself.

Now one day, as he and his goats were crossing the King's Highway, the Princess happened to be approaching in her carriage.

"Make way! Make way for the Princess!" cried her outriders, so the Goatherd, herding his flock to the side of the road, stood respectfully back.

The Princess, who had been sleeping, was wakened by the noise, and curious, she pulled aside her curtains just in time to gaze straight into the eyes of the Goatherd. Never had the Princess imagined such eyes. Were they brown or were they gold? She could hardly tell. But they were more beautiful than any she had ever seen and they looked right into her heart.

And never had the Goatherd imagined such beauty. A newborn doe, a pearly sunrise in the mountains, wild flowers in the meadow—these were all beautiful things, and each time he saw them his heart turned over. But the Princess was more beautiful still. Her hair was black and glossy as a raven's feathers and her eyes—how could he have known that eyes could be so large and so blue? Although he had seen her for no more than a passing second, he stood dazed, rooted to the spot, staring after her carriage until it was out of sight.

From that moment the Goatherd's life changed. The face of the Princess filled his dreams; it accompanied him on his walks to the high pastures. Where once he had seen flowers and the first small strawberries, now he saw only the Princess. Waking or sleeping he could think only of her.

Finally—unable to bear his life without her, and determined to see her one more time—he left his goats in the care of a trusted friend, slung his goatskin over his shoulder and set out on the long, hard road to the Palace.

II

Behind the tall and turreted walls of the Palace grounds the Princess paced back and forth in her private garden.

It was a beautiful garden. Peacocks strutted across its smooth green lawns. Fountains sprinkled drops of water like glittering jewels. Lilies, lady slippers, and shooting stars grew among the blue-eyed grasses near the pool. Butterflies— orange and yellow and white and black—fluttered from flower to flower. The air was heady with scents of cinnamon, clove, and apricots. Bright birds sang.

But the Princess walked as in a trance. Ever since she had gazed into the eyes of the Goatherd, she had been unable to think of anyone else. She knew the Goatherd was the only man she would ever consent to marry and, by the laws of the Kingdom, it was time for her to choose a husband. But she feared her father would not approve of her choice. So the Princess grieved and tears fell from her beautiful eyes.

"Do not cry, dear Princess," the voice of her Fairy Godmother came suddenly out of nowhere.

"Oh, how glad I am to hear you!" cried the unhappy Princess, cheering up a little. "Did you know how much I needed you?"

"I always know when you are sad," said the Fairy Godmother. "It makes my eyes water. In fact, I even know why you are sad. You are thinking of the Goatherd. But listen carefully—I have a plan. I have suggested to your father that you will agree to marry the first citizen of Ure to present the Court with a flask of sea water."

"Sea water!" exclaimed the Princess in astonishment, for only members of the Royal Family had ever reached the sea. "Sea water! Oh-h-h, but I wouldn't marry anyone but the Goatherd—not if he were to bring me a hundred flasks."

"But if it were the Goatherd . . . ?" said the Godmother and the Princess was quietened by the tone of her voice.

"As I said, I have a plan, but it will succeed only with your help. You must give me your word that you will never for a moment doubt that all will be well in the end, even when things seem to be going very badly or—worse—*when nothing seems to be happening at all.* This will be more difficult than you think. In fact, there will be times when it will be very difficult indeed. But you must try," said the Fairy Godmother. "It's our only hope."

"Oh, I *will!*" said the now thoughtful Princess, "With all my heart!"

III

The Kingdom of Ure, you will remember, is a land-locked kingdom and none but members of the Royal Family *had* ever reached the sea. In fact, many of its inhabitants had never even heard of it. Of those who had, most were not interested, while others thought of it as nothing more than a tale told to rambunctious children—for the sea was reported to say *soowish-soowish*, a sound known to have a mysterious soothing effect.

Some legends told of travellers who had set out in search of it and never returned; others claimed it teemed with terrifying monsters. And who could seriously believe in something that was variously described as grey, or green, or blue—or as smooth as a millpond, or filled with mountainous peaks?

When the Palace announced that the Princess would marry the first man to return with a flask of sea water, every unmarried man in the Kingdom was eager to compete, for the winner would not only marry the Princess, he would reign with her when the old King died. But after considering the difficulties of the task ahead, many decided that the girl next door had grown remarkably attractive lately and, on second thought, that kingly duties would be nothing but a burden and a bore.

Finally, there were only three young men in all the land who resolved to win the Princess—Stabdyl, Mungu and a dusty young Goatherd no one had ever seen before who arrived outside the Palace gates just as the announcement was proclaimed.

Stabdyl was well-known in Ure. He was the reckless and idle son of one of the King's advisors. He had no wish to marry the Princess or anyone else, but his father, who recognized the advantage of having the Princess as his daughter-in-law, persuaded his son to enter the contest by offering him the fastest horse in the Kingdom.

Mungu, vain and ambitious, was stepson of the King's cousin, and his heart was set on the throne. In preparation for the contest, and as befitted one destined to be King, he equipped himself with a fine steed and a mounted servant to carry his belongings—all, that is, but the beautiful cut-glass flask in which to bring back the sea water. That he would carry himself.

The Goatherd, dusty and weary, had arrived at the Palace Gate with a single wish in his heart: to see the Princess one more time. But when he learned that with a flask of sea water he could not only see her again but might even win her hand, he put his mind to work. With what remained of his money, he bought a pair of stout boots for the journey. And because he was far from stupid, he knew he should find out everything he could about the sea before setting forth in search of it. To this end he listened attentively to talk in the town and asked questions whenever possible. But the answers he received were so contradictory that he found himself more confused than before he began. As to where the sea was, or how he would recognize it, nobody knew. Nobody, that is, but the King and the Princess and he could not ask them.

Stabdyl and Mungu set forth from the capital to the waving of flags and the flourish of trumpets. But the Goatherd, poor and friendless, had no one to see him off. Nor was he in any great hurry to leave, for if speed were necessary to win the Princess, he—without a horse—was already doomed. So instead of following behind in the dust, he set off for the Palace, hoping to catch one final glimpse of the Princess before he left.

No sooner had he arrived outside the Palace wall than he saw an old Beggar Woman who, to his surprise, grabbed him by the arm and pushed him through a small gate.

Inside was a garden unlike anything he had ever seen—green velvet lawns, fruit-laden trees, and birdsong so sweet that he stopped, stock-still, to listen. And then, rounding the corner of a little pavilion, came the Princess herself.

The Goatherd's heart skipped a beat and he was quite speechless when he flung himself on his knees at her feet. But the Princess took his hand in hers and bade him stand and as she looked deep into his eyes he saw that her gaze was even bluer and more beautiful than he remembered; and her fingers trembled in his as they stood for a minute or an hour—how could they tell?—before he drew her to him and held her against his breast.

"You must go now," she said at last. "You must delay no longer. But before you go, you must tell me your name."

"I am the Goatherd," replied the Goatherd.

"No, your *name*" laughed the Princess. "Herding goats is what you *do*. What do they *call* you?"

"They call me the Goatherd, or just—Goatherd," he replied, not understanding.

"But you must have a name," she said. "I shall give you one," and she shut her eyes and crinkled her delicious nose in thought. And then, "Galaad," she said. "I shall call you Galaad, because it rhymes with glad. Now go, Galaad, and take this for your journey," and she took from around her neck a golden locket, which she slipped over his head.

"Travel light," she went on, "for it is a long journey. And never doubt that you will find the sea in the end. As to what it is like, I think you will know it when you see it. It is wide as the skies and blue as my eyes." She led him quickly to the little gate, pressed her lips to his and lifted the latch.

The Goatherd was once again on the city street, but now he had a name—Galaad—which the Princess had given him, and her beautiful golden locket, and he knew a little bit more about the sea.

IV

Stabdyl, when he set out from the capital, travelled east across the rolling plains, for only there could he gallop his horse. In fact, he travelled so fast that at the end of the first day's journey he and his fiery steed were exhausted and could go no further. Stopping at a lonely hut, he asked shelter of the Old Woman who opened the door.

"Come in, come in," the Old Woman said. "But your horse is in a lather, fine sir, and I have no servant to rub it down. If you can look after it yourself, I'll be about making your bed and heating some broth for your supper."

"I'm tired, Old Woman," Stabdyl replied. "Let me eat the soup first and I'll attend to my horse later." And so Stabdyl tied his poor horse to a tree and went inside and greedily drank the soup. Then he fell fast asleep.

When he awoke in the morning and remembered that he had to be first at the sea, he called for his breakfast.

"I have just enough wood to heat the porridge," the Old Woman said. "Would you split me a few sticks of kindling before you go on your way?"

But Stabdyl was in too great a hurry. He gobbled his porridge and, barely thanking the Old Woman for her hospitality, saddled his horse, leaped onto its back and touched his spurs to its ribs. But the fastest horse in the Kingdom stood stock-still. Neither his spurs nor his whip made the least difference.

Enraged, Stabdyl jumped to the ground and pulled on the bridle but pull as he would, the horse refused to budge. "All right, then," he cried in a rage. "Stay where you are. I'll go on foot."

Before long he discovered that his beautiful boots, handsomely tooled and fine in stirrups, were ill-suited to walking. In no time at all, his feet were blistered and sore and he had to sit down and bathe them in a stream.

"More haste, less speed, Stabdyl," said a small voice nearby.

Stabdyl looked around but all he could see were the beady little eyes of a field mouse. Now Stabdyl knew perfectly well that mice can't talk but as he stared at this one he saw quite clearly that the voice was coming from its tiny mouth. Nevertheless, he said, "Mice can't talk."

"Of course not," said the mouse.

"Then why are you talking?"

"Just passing the time of day, as a courteous field mouse should," the mouse replied.

"Do you live around here?" Stabdyl inquired.

"Around here, around there," answered the mouse, gesturing widely.

"Then perhaps," said Stabdyl eagerly, "you have seen the sea in your travels."

"Indeed," said the field mouse, "and of course."

"Could you—lead me to it?" asked Stabdyl, getting to his feet.

"I could," said the field mouse.

"Then let us make haste," said Stabdyl. He had forgotten his sore feet.

"I said I *could*, I didn't say I *would*." The mouse came close to Stabdyl. "In fact," he began, whereupon he ran fearlessly up Stabdyl's trouser leg and disappeared into the pouch than hung from Stabdyl's belt. From there the rest of the mouse's sentence sounded like nothing more than so much squeaking, which Stabdyl couldn't understand at all.

Stabdyl grew impatient. "I am in a great hurry," he said, speaking into his pouch. "A very GREAT HURRY. And if, as you say, you know the way to the sea, then take me to it. There is no time to lose."

"Time to lose?" said the field mouse, popping his head over the edge of the pouch. "Who ever heard of losing time? Here we find time. We never lose it."

"It must have been lost once in order for you to find it," Stabdyl retorted, drawn into the argument in spite of himself. And then, becoming impatient, "If you're so good at finding time, then please be kind enough to find enough to take me to the sea."

"We shall have to look for it then," said the field mouse calmly. "Would you be so good as to help?" And he ran down Stabdyl's leg and began peering behind rocks in a quite methodical way.

"The larger rocks," he said, "you can handle better than I, and I'd be greatly obliged . . ."

Stabdyl was near the end of his politeness but he couldn't afford

to lose his guide to the sea and so he began, with not very good grace, to move the large rocks and look under them.

"Do you usually find time under rocks?" he asked.

"As a matter of fact," said the mouse, continuing his search, "it has never been found there before. But you simply don't know where you'll find it next. Here one day, there another."

Just as Stabdyl had decided he would do better to go on his way alone, the field mouse squeaked, "Eureka! A good-sized piece! What luck! Quite enough to take us to the sea, if we hurry." And with that he set off at a quick, skittering run.

Following him proved difficult, for the mouse could go where Stabdyl could not. At times Stabdyl thought he had lost the mouse entirely. But finally, after many detours, disappearances, and re-unions, the mouse cried out, "We're getting close!"

Stabdyl strained his ears for the *soowish-soowish* the old tales had led him to expect, but all he could hear were sucking sounds made by his bare feet in marshy ground. Yet he began to be excited at the thought of reaching the sea and he felt grateful to the mouse. Then he congratulated himself on how clever *he* had been and before long he had convinced himself that his success was due entirely to his own resourcefulness and skill. And he saw himself winning the hand of the Princess and leading a life of luxury and leisure, his stables filled with the finest horses. But to the Princess herself he gave no thought at all.

"We'll just about make it," cried the mouse, breaking into Stabdyl's reverie.

"Make what?"

"Make it to the sea, of course," the mouse said as patiently as possible. "I only found a medium-sized piece of time, you know, and what with your slowness and one thing and another, I began to wonder if we would."

At that moment they came out from a clump of swamp alder and "Voilà!" cried the mouse, gesturing with a rather muddy paw.

Stabdyl looked across the wide expanse of shallow water, at the reeds and rushes growing at its edges, at the pink and yellow lilies floating on its smooth surface. Then, heart pounding in his chest, hand shaking with excitement, Stabdyl stooped and carefully filled his flask.

V

Having watched Stabyl gallop eastward, Mungu accompanied by his mounted servant, spurred his own steed and turned its head to the west. His plan was to ride directly to the high mountains from whose topmost crests he believed he would be able to see the sea.

When darkness fell, Mungu's servant pitched a fine silken tent for his master to sleep in. At dawn they broke camp and worked their horses up the dangerous rocky track. A week passed in this manner. It grew colder as they climbed. The air became harder to breathe. Their horses moved more and more slowly.

One day the servant, who was an old man, could go no further. Mungu gave him orders to return home on foot.

Astride his own horse, his servant's poor beast now loaded with all his possessions, Mungu struggled on. Had it not been for his dream of the crown, he could not have borne such hardship.

At length, weary—and hungry too, for his food was running low— he came to the high pass from which he hoped to have a distant view of the sea. But dense cloud filled the air and he could see no more than a few yards ahead of him. Mungu was about to force his horses on when he noticed a cave in the rock and within it, sitting as if carved, an extraordinary figure. The figure's hair and beard were white as icicles. In one hand he held a shell—something Mungu had never seen before—and his eyes, the only part of him that looked alive, blazed like blue fire.

Apart from his horses and the occasional mountain goat, Mungu had seen no living thing for several days, so he stared at the figure as if it were a vision. Then in the silence and out of his terrible loneliness Mungu said, "I am tired and I am cold and I am looking for the sea."

"The Western Sea?" the Old Man inquired. "You are a long way from the sea, my son."

"How far?" asked Mungu.

"Farther than you think," the Old Man said.

"Old Man," said Mungu and his voice was hard, "I have to reach the sea. If you know where it is and how far away it is, perhaps you can give me some help."

"I could give you help," the Old Man replied, "but I don't think you would accept it."

"*I must reach the sea!*" said Mungu again.

"Very well," said the Old Man. "I have three pieces of advice. The first, that you leave your horses with me."

"Leave my *horses!*" shouted Mungu. "But my horses are my only means of transportation."

"The second," went on the Old Man as if Mungu had not spoken, "that you leave your saddle-bags with me."

"Never!" cried Mungu. "My saddle-bags hold everything I own, including my beautiful cut-glass flask in which to carry home the sea water."

"And third," said the Old Man, "that you leave your cut-glass flask."

"You would be happy to own all my belongings, wouldn't you, you ragged old beggar," cried Mungu in a fury. "You could sell my horses and my silken tent and my golden dishes and my beautiful cut-glass flask, couldn't you? No, Old Man. I am not such a fool as you think."

But suddenly the Old Man didn't look like a beggar at all. His ragged clothing gave off a blinding light, his eyes shone like frosty stars and Mungu's blood ran freezing through his veins. He was more afraid than he had ever been in his life before and he urged his horses on.

That night, as Mungu was camped on a narrow ledge—too narrow for him to pitch his silken tent—his fine horse missed its footing in the dark and dropped down the sheer face of the mountain.

"Oh, clumsy horse! Oh, careless, stupid horse!" cried Mungu in a fury, clenching his fists and shaking them at the stars. "What in the name of the Crown am I going to do?"

Fearful that his other horse might meet the same fate, taking all his possessions with it, Mungu in desperation, decided to carry the saddle-bags himself. Burdened now by his many belongings which grew heavier and heavier, stumbling often, nearly falling, he and his servant's horse picked their way down the narrow, rocky trail.

Mungu soon found that it was impossible to continue in this way. Reluctantly he began throwing his things away. First to go was his beautiful silken tent; next his golden dishes; then his purple velvet cloak, his green brocade trousers, his richly tooled boots, and the many lengths of coloured silks to tie his turbans. But Mungu's heart was heavy and the steep slope down which he struggled was slippery and treacherous in the rain.

Then one morning, when Mungu had almost forgotten the sun, he awakened to its light. For the first time since crossing the height of land he could see more than a few feet ahead of him. Anxiously he searched the horizon for the sea, but all he could see were rolling foothills, rolling forever and ever.

Mungu remembered the words of the Old Man in the cave, "You are a long way from the sea, my son." And he began to wonder, as many of his countrymen had before him, if the sea were no more than a fable, after all.

But the dream of being King drove him on.

By the time he reached the grasslands, Mungu had nothing but

his horse, the clothes he stood up in, and his beautiful cut-glass flask. The horse he decided to leave behind. After so terrible a journey it was mere skin and bone. He would make better time on foot.

At night, with nothing to shelter him from the weather, he lay down under the stars. His sight became sharp from looking for wild berries and there was a crazed look in his eyes. He grew thin and strong as steel and as he walked on in search of the sea he made plans for when he would be king. His plans would not have pleased the citizens of Ure.

Then, one day when he was bending over a rushing stream to drink, his beautiful cut-glass flask slipped from his bag and was dashed to pieces on the rocks.

For the first time in his long, hard journey, Mungu sank down in despair and buried his head in his hands.

VI

Galaad, if you remember, set out from the capital of Ure with a light heart. He wore the Princess's locket around his neck and her words still rang in his ears.

Like Stabdyl before him, he set off towards the east. And like Stabdyl, he too, came to the hut of the Old Woman, who made him soup and gave him a bed. It was the first bed Galaad had slept in since leaving his own village so he awakened refreshed and grateful.

"What can I do for you in return for your hospitality, Mother?" Galaad asked after breakfast.

"Oh, young master, if you could split me some wood," the Old Woman said, "for truly, I am past it."

And so Galaad set to and split a large pile of wood. And when he had stacked it neatly and was about to go on his way, the Old Woman said, "And if you could draw me some water, young master, I would be very pleased."

And so Galaad set to and drew seven buckets of water, one for each day of the week. And when he had finished the Old Woman said, "Young master, it's a long time since anyone has passed this way with a willing heart and who knows when anyone will again—and my roof is badly in need of repair."

And so Galaad set to and mended the roof and filled the floor boards and the cracks around doors and windows until at last the house was as snug as a house can be. And when he had finished, the

Old Woman said, "You have looked after me like a son. Go now, and may success go with you."

And then she reached into her apron pocket and brought forth a smooth stone—as black and as shiny as the Princess's hair. "Take this," she said and she put it in his palm where it lay heavy for its size, and warm. "It was given to me many years ago and it is said to grant one wish to each owner. I never used it until last week when I wished for a strong young man who would look after me as if he were my son. Today it granted my wish. Now, it is yours. Use it only when all else fails."

Galaad put the stone in his pouch, embraced the Old Woman and went on his way with a light heart.

Before he had gone very far he heard a small voice saying, "Are you looking for the sea, too?" And there was a field mouse sitting on a log.

"Too?" asked Galaad. "Have there been others?"

"One other," the mouse replied. "And I took him to the sea and he filled a bottle with water to win the hand of a Princess. But why she would want a bottle of sea water, I can't imagine."

Galaad's heart fell. If someone had been to the sea before him, what point was there in going on? But at the thought of the Princess he knew he must never give up.

"Would you take me to the sea?" he asked the mouse. "Now."

"Willingly," the mouse replied. And once again he led the way along the stream until they came to the same expanse of water with reeds and rushes growing at its edges and water lilies floating on its smooth surface.

"As wide as the skies and as blue as her eyes," Galaad said to himself. And it did, indeed, seem to fit the description. Almost, that is. It was not quite as wide as the skies but it was a large body of water, larger than any that Galaad had ever seen.

As he bent down to fill his goatskin he said to himself, "If I return with all speed, perhaps I can still arrive first at the Palace." And thanking the mouse for his help Galaad began the journey back to the capital.

Almost at once he came across a man sitting by the roadside. "Water. Water," the man croaked, pointing to his mouth. So Galaad unstoppered his goatskin and handed it to the thirsty man who drank and drank and drank until there was no drop left.

"Are you better, Father?" Galaad inquired. "Because, if so, I must return to the sea to refill my goatskin, for without sea water I cannot win the hand of the Princess whom I love."

"Sea water!" laughed the man. "Where do you come from, boy, that you think that was sea water? Why, no one can drink sea water. It's too salty."

"Salty?" said Galaad and his eyes widened and his heart lightened.

"Salty as a kipper," the man said cheerfully. "Salty as an anchovy."

Galaad who had never heard of either kippers or anchovies asked, just to make absolutely certain, "As salty as—salt?"

"If you wish," said the man. "As salty as salt. As salty as tears."

"As wide as the skies, as blue as her eyes, and as salty as tears. It's not a very good *rhyme*," Galaad said, "but it does help with the description."

Then the man took from his pouch a beautiful shell, such as Galaad had never seen, and he held it to Galaad's ear so that he could hear the *soowish-soowish* of the sea.

"As wide as the skies, as blue as her eyes, as salty as tears, and with shells on its shores," the man said, adding, "And it's no great distance from here at all, at all, the sea isn't. Why, this road you're on leads directly to it."

So, once again, grateful and full of thanks, Galaad set off in search of the sea.

VII

Meanwhile, in the Kingdom of Ure, husbands told wives and wives told children that Stabdyl was on his way home with a flask of sea water. So fast, in fact, did the news travel that it reached the capital ahead of Stabdyl himself. And great was the rejoicing, for everyone looked forward to the celebrations which accompany a royal wedding . . . everyone, that is, but the Princess, who was finding it very hard to remember that all would be well in the end.

Outside the Palace an excited crowd awaited the arrival of Stabdyl. And when, at last, he appeared—bathed, scented, and dressed in his finest clothes, with the sea water in its silver flask carried on a velvet cushion—a joyous cry arose to greet him.

Inside the Palace the King sat on his golden throne; by his side the Princess, deathly pale; and, more than usually prominent, the King's advisor, father of Stabdyl, who already thought of the Princess as his daughter-in-law.

Stabdyl, with barely a glance at the Princess, his mind on fire with the dream of fast horses, stepped forward and presented his flask to the King. To the astonishment of the Court, the King unstoppered the flask and put it to his lips as if to drink it.

"This is not sea water," the King said.

"Not sea water!" cried the King's advisor, his voice quavering.

"But, your Majesty," protested Stabdyl, "I filled the flask with my own hands. From the sea itself."

"What makes you think it was the sea?" the King inquired.

"I travelled many miles," Stabdyl replied. "Miles and miles with no sight of the sea. Then, when I had nearly given up hope, I met a mouse. He led me to the sea."

"A mouse?" asked the King and all the courtiers echoed their Monarch. "A mouse?" "A mou-ouse?" A MOUse!" "A MOUSE!"

"A mouse," Stabdyl repeated, feeling now rather foolish.

"I think it may be generally assumed," said the King, "that if a mouse leads you to the sea, it will be a mouse's sea, not a man's. This water, I conclude, is from a pond. Possibly one with reeds and rushes growing at its edges and lilies floating where its shallows are."

Anyone watching the King's advisor would have seen the colour leave his cheeks at these words. And anyone watching the Princess would have seen the colour return to hers.

As for Stabdyl, he felt a pang of disappointment as the fast horses of which he had dreamed, slipped from his grasp. But he was not one to waste time on regrets. Already he was thinking of other ways to amuse himself.

VIII

Galaad, now sure of his way, followed the road the man said led directly to the sea. He knew that he had been saved from returning to the Court with a goatskin of pond water. But what he did not know was that he was crossing lands owned by the Wizard of the Eastern Seaboard.

He had travelled no distance at all before storm clouds filled the sky and the bright day darkened. Lightning crackled overhead, distant thunder rolled. Rain came down in sheets. A nearby house offered promise of shelter and when Galaad knocked on its door, a servant answered.

"May I take shelter from the rain?" Galaad asked. "It's a bad time to be out on foot."

"My master does not like visitors," the servant replied. "But he is away on business and I could do with a bit of human company."

He led Galaad down a long dark corridor. Behind shut doors on either side Galaad could hear dogs barking and cats meowing and horses neighing and goats bleating. He had worked too long as a goatherd not to know an unhappy goat when he heard one. And he didn't think the other animals sounded too happy either.

"What a lot of animals your master owns," said Galaad.

"Aye," replied the servant, "that he does. And I reckon he will own one more by nightfall."

Then he ushered Galaad into the kitchen and took his wet clothes and gave him a steaming cup of mead, sweet and soothing. Galaad drank it gratefully and slipped off at once into a deep sleep.

"Ha ha!" said the servant rubbing his hands gleefully. "One more by nightfall. My master will be pleased when he comes home."

"Ha ha!" said the Wizard returning home, "has my good servant caught another human being with his honey? Has he indeed! What shall we turn him into, my man? I've not done a goat for a very long time. I think I'll turn him into a goat."

The Wizard was a tall man in a long coat with trailing sleeves and eyes as black as licorice.

"Thinks he can cross my land, does he?" he asked of the air as he passed his fingers over and around the sleeping Galaad.

"On second thought," he went on and his fingers traced a slower and more complicated design, "I think I'll make him into a goatherd. He can look after my goats."

He began a jerky dance around Galaad and his voice became cold and hard as he said, "You will forget everything that has ever happened to you. Abracadabra. You will forget your own name and your own mission. Abracadabra. All you will know are my goats. Forever . . . and ever . . . and ever."

And such was the power of the Wizard's spell that Galaad indeed forgot everything. He forgot that he was in search of the sea. He forgot his own name. He even forgot the Princess.

IX

Now the Wizard was interested in Galaad for political reasons. He had long been an enemy of the King of Ure who refused to make war with him against neighbouring states. So when he had heard that the Princess was about to marry, he made it a point to find out everything he could about the three suitors.

Stabdyl, he discovered, was a greedy and idle boy, always in a hurry and of no conceivable use to him. Galaad clearly would follow in the footsteps of the old King and so he must not be allowed to

marry the Princess. But Mungu was vain and ambitious and greedy and cruel—just the kind of accomplice the Wizard needed.

With Stabdyl out of the running and Galaad busy with the goats, the Wizard could give his full attention to Mungu. Not that it was going to prove as easy as he'd hoped, for Mungu was on the other side of the continent, wandering half-crazed in the direction of the Western Sea—a region where the Wizard's powers were greatly reduced. Although he could assist Mungu in bringing about Mungu's own desires, he was completely unable to put ideas or wishes in Mungu's head. And the trouble with Mungu at the moment was that he had fallen into a terrible aimlessness and only at times remembered why he had set out on his endless journey. So all the Wizard could do was wait.

Then one morning Mungu awakened and thought of the flask of sea water, without which his dream could never come true. And he thought of the Western Sea which the Old Man in the cave had spoken of those many long months ago. And no sooner had the thought entered his mind than the Wizard deposited him on its golden shore.

Dazed, Mungu stared at the sweep of blue water, vaster and more blue than anything he had ever imagined. Then he fell on his knees and tried to drink, but the salt on his lips and throat was like fire and he ran back from the sea as if burned and once again he forgot the crown and the Wizard could only wait.

When at last Mungu realized that this water was, in fact, the very sea for which he had been searching, he was desperate to find a container, fill it, and return to the Kingdom of Ure with all speed. So the Wizard, invisible as air, directed Mungu to a stoppered bottle which lay, half-hidden in a tangle of seaweed.

Now everyone knows that a stoppered bottle may well contain a genie—everyone, that is, but Mungu who, with only one idea in his head and no thought at all of possible consequences, pulled on the stopper with all his strength.

In a flash, an immense figure rose like smoke from the bottle, towering over the astonished Mungu and frightening him half to death. But to his surprise, the ferocious-looking creature bowed low and said in a voice so loud Mungu had to put his hands over his ears, "Command me!"

Without hesitation, eyes blazing, greed bursting his heart, Mungu cried out in a great voice, almost a match for the genie's, "Make me King!"

X

The Wizard was well content with the spell he had put on Galaad, for Galaad had forgotten everything. Day after day he took the Wizard's goats to pasture and night after night he brought them home again. No thought of the Princess or the sea ever entered his head. And so he might have gone on forever had he not met the same Old Women who had pushed him into the Princess's garden. Not that he recognized her. The Wizard had seen to that.

"Young man," she begged, "I am poor and you are rich. Give me one of your goats."

"I am sorry, Mother," Galaad replied. "I can't give you a goat, for the goats are not mine. I am only a poor goatherd with nothing to give you at all."

"How can I believe what you tell me when you wear that beautiful golden locket around your neck?"

"Golden locket?" said Galaad, who had forgotten all about it. "I have no locket." But when he put his hand to his neck he found that he had.

"If the goats are not yours, the locket is. You could give me the locket," the Old Woman said.

"Old Woman," Galaad replied, "I wish I could give you something that would be of use to you. But I cannot give you the locket."

"You don't care about a poor old woman at all," she whined. "Why can't you give it to me, if it is yours?"

Now Galaad didn't know why he couldn't give her the locket. All he knew was that it gave him a feeling so sweet, so half-forgotten, that he wanted nothing more than to hold it in his hand and stare at it.

"How is it a poor goatherd can own a golden locket?" the Old Woman went on, sidling up to him and looking at him suspiciously. "Perhaps," she said, "you stole it. Heh-heh-heh." And she laughed a nasty laugh.

"Oh, no," said Galaad, horrified. "I didn't steal it." But poor Galaad was not even certain of that, for there was nothing but a blank in his head when he tried to remember where it came from.

"Aha!" the Old Woman exclaimed as she took the locket in her hand and turned it over, "you must have stolen it right enough. And from the Princess, too. See, here is the Royal Seal."

"The Princess?" cried Galaad and his heart leaped. "The Princess? What Princess, Old Woman?"

"The Princess of Ure who, at this very moment, is expecting one

of her suitors to return with a flask of sea water."

"Sea water!" said Galaad. And as he uttered those words the spell broke. All memory came rushing back. He remembered the mountain meadows outside his village and the first glimpse he had had of the Princess; he remembered his meeting with the Princess in the garden when she gave him his name and her locket. He remembered his search for the sea. And he knew that what he should be doing now was continuing that search and not wasting time on goats and old women— for Galaad didn't realize that this was the same Old Woman who had helped him before and that it was thanks to her that the Wizard's spell was now undone.

"You must excuse me, Mother," said Galaad. "I have just remembered something very important."

"Not so fast, not so fast," the Old Woman cautioned. "You are planning to go to the sea. But if you abandon the goats the Wizard, under whose spell you have been, will know at once that you are free of it. On his land he is a powerful magician and can cast a spell stronger than stone."

Galaad looked at the Old Woman in amazement. How did she know that he was planning to go to the sea?

"You are wondering if I can read your mind," she went on. "Well, I can. Now listen. I have a plan. Go home tonight as usual. Then tomorrow morning when you take your goats to pasture, drive them due east without stopping. By midday you should be at the sea. Fill your goatskin with sea water and walk south along the shore. On the shore you are safe. Below the high-tide mark the Wizard has no power over you. You will come, at last, to a great headland jutting into the ocean, and here you will have to be extremely careful, for this headland cannot be climbed. From there, the only way to Ure is across the Wizard's land. It is not a long way but it is full of dangers. You will have to have all your wits about you for this last part of the journey."

Suddenly it came to Galaad that this was the same Old Woman who had helped him before. "Who are you, Old Woman?" he asked. But he asked the question of the air. The Old Woman had disappeared as if she had never been.

XI

Galaad did as the Old Woman advised. He drove his goats home to the Wizard's house in the evening, ate his bread and water, and went to bed in the stable. When morning broke, he was already on his way due east. And as the sun stood at mid-point in the sky, Galaad smelled a totally new smell—tangy and delicious and invigorating; and mounting a low sandy hillock, he saw before him, "wide as the skies and blue as her eyes" what could only be the sea. Sparkling sapphire water stretched in three directions and where it met the shore it broke in foam as white as the lace at the neck and wrists of the Princess's dress. And where the foam dissolved and disappeared in the sand, it left an irregular line of glistening shells.

With a loud cry that drove his goats forward, Galaad raced into the healing waves and in his heart there was no doubt at all that he had, at last, arrived at the sea. And it was more beautiful even than he had dreamed.

Then above the *soowish-soowish* of its waters he heard great joyful cries and, turning, he saw that the goats had changed into young men and women who came splashing towards him, calling out their thanks that they were free of the goat bodies into which the Wizard had locked them.

And then Galaad remembered the Princess. He bent and filled his goatskin with sea water, and as he did so it changed to a beautiful golden flask. And he saw that his clothing too, instead of being the simple homespun of a goatherd, was changed into velvets and brocades like the garments of a prince.

But the advice of the Old Woman sounded in his ears and he called to his new-found companions to follow him, warning them that they were only safe from the enchantments of the Wizard if they stayed below the high-tide line.

"Keep close together and follow me," he cautioned as they stopped to pick up shells, to make chains of seaweed, or to play in the sparkling waters. Once or twice he was tempted to go on without them but each time a heavy weight fell upon his heart and he knew that he must take them with him.

And so, with many stops and starts, they travelled on together until they arrived at the great unscalable headland where they must cross the Wizard's land. And Galaad knew that of all the trials he had so far faced, this—because he knew about it in advance—was the worst. He called his friends together and warned them of the dangers ahead.

What he saw, when he climbed a high rock to survey the Wizard's land, was a flower-filled meadow, golden in the late afternoon sun—as innocent-appearing a meadow as you could wish to see. And beyond, at no great distance, the majestic mountains of Ure.

While he stood, considering the time it would take them to reach

the mountains, one of the young men ran up from the sands, hand out-stretched, to pick a wild rose. But before he could pluck it from its bush, he was a goat again. And all the young men and women on the shore cried out in fear of the Wizard.

Then Galaad remembered the stone that could grant him one wish and he pulled it from his pouch. Holding it firmly in his fist and thinking fast but very carefully, he wished: "Carry us all safely to the Kingdom of Ure—including the goat."

No sooner had he spoken than it was as if they were lifted in the folds of an invisible cloak and carried high into the air, skirts and shirt-tails and hair blowing out about them and the poor goat bleating pitifully as he tipped and titled in his sudden flight.

In no more time than it takes to tell, they arrived safely in the Kingdom of Ure. Galaad, stopping only to bathe and brush the sand from his hair, took his beautiful golden flask of sea water to the Palace where he presented it to the King. And when the King had put it to his lips to make sure it was truly sea water, he gave Galaad the Princess's hand in marriage.

For the wedding everyone wore their best clothes and there was a great feast and the dancing continued for weeks. Next to the Princess, the most beautiful of all was the Fairy Godmother, dressed at last in her rightful clothes of gossamer and looking almost as young as the Princess herself. But whenever Galaad looked into her eyes, he couldn't help being reminded of the old women who had helped him in his travels—and even the old man.

XII

And Mungu? Mungu was so greedy to be King, if you remember, and in so great a hurry, that he forgot to ask the genie to make him King of Ure. And the only kingdom without a king at the moment he made his wish was a rocky, wind-swept island a thousand miles away. And there Mungu is monarch and he thinks and he thinks and he thinks.

And the goat? Oh, yes, the goat! But that is another story.

A Note from the Author

All my life, I have loved fairy tales. When young, I was lucky enough to have parents who read them to me—parents who loved them too. Now that I am older, I approach them less literally and respond to them more deeply. They are tales of hope. They show me unexpected things about myself and the world. They are rich in reminders of perseverance and kindliness. And, even more important, they persuade me that another, invisible world can manifest itself within our three-dimensional, daily one.

In the light of all this, it is not surprising that I should want to write a fairy story myself—a traditional fairy story. But I was never able to do so. And then, one night, the phrase "blue blood" came into my head. Webster defines it—and I quote—as "membership in a noble or socially prominent family". The Shorter Oxford—to quote again—says, "tr. Sp. *sangre azul* claimed by certain families of Castile as being uncontaminated [*sic*] by Moorish, Jewish or other admixture; probably founded on the blueness of the veins of people of fair complexion."

"Blue blood"—*sea-blue blood*, so my idle thoughts ran. But, of course! Why hadn't I seen it before? "Blue blood" had nothing to do with class or race. It was a term applied to the wise, to those who, symbolically, had been to the sea—that mythical source of all life, the "great mother", which, in most cultures, represents wisdom, wholeness, truth—and as a result, in whose veins flowed, symbolically again, blood that was (sea) blue.

And as for Royalty being "blue-blooded"—(royal blue, note!)—perhaps, in some Golden Age, "blue blood" had nothing to do with lineage and everything to do with wisdom; and that in seeking his successor, the old King in the fairy tales was trying to find a young man as wise or, in my terminology, as "blue-blooded" as he. I can't think of a single tale in which the Kingdom *automatically* goes to the rightful heir.

But I am no scholar. I am no etymologist either, and I am not trying to persuade you of the rightness of my notion. Perhaps there was no Golden Age when kings were chosen for their wisdom—perhaps that happens only in fairy tales. But, interestingly, on checking four historically wise rulers, I found that three—Solomon, Alexander the Great, and Charlemagne—had no clear titles to the kingdoms they ruled, and that the fourth—Haroun el-Rashid, Charlemagne's friend—had a curiously unconventional line of ascent.

So that is where my ruminations about "blue blood" led me; and how I came to write a traditional fairy tale in which a young man, in order to win the hand of the Princess, made the long and difficult journey to the sea. In so doing, he proved himself a wise and worthy successor to the old King.